The Diary

of

Robin's Toys

Ken and Angie Lake

1

2

Carlos the Cod

Published by Sweet Cherry Publishing Limited
53 St. Stephens Road,
Leicester, LE2 1GH
United Kingdom

First Published in the UK in 2013

ISBN: 978-1-78226-023-3
Text: © Ken and Angie Lake 2013
Illustrations: (c) Vishnu Madhav,
Creative Books

Title: Carlos the Cod - The Diaries of Robin's Toys

Printed and Bound By Nutech Print Services, India

Every Toy Has a Story to Tell

Have you ever seen an old toy, perhaps in a cupboard, or in the attic or loft? Have you ever seen how sad they look at car boot sales, unwanted and unloved? Well, look at them closely, because every toy has a story to tell, and the older, the more decrepit, the more scruffy, the more tatty the toy is, the more interesting its story could be. Here are just a few of those toys and their stories.

8th April, 09.20

It was Sunday morning, and Robin stared blankly through the rain-soaked window, down the wet and almost deserted street.

Splish, splash, splish, splash. The rain poured over the house guttering and ran down the street in little streams, forming puddles with rainbow colours floating on the surface.

Why does it have to rain on Sundays? he thought. *It's not fair.* Sunday was Robin's day out with his grandad at the car boot sale, but now it was sure to be cancelled.

As he watched and waited, a big blue car drove down the street. It splashed through the puddles and sprayed water all over the paperboy. He shouted something and waved his fist at the driver. Mr Jones at number 9 would be getting a wet newspaper this morning.

A young girl was trying to light a cigarette in the rain. Robin wondered why people smoked; he knew that it was bad for them and cost them a lot of money.

He just didn't understand it. Just as she seemed to get it to light, another car drove past and splashed water all over her.

She shouted something at the driver and threw the wet cigarette away.

The sad, gloomy weather suited Robin's mood perfectly. Just yesterday afternoon his friend Angus was supposed to come round to play, but he hadn't shown up. Robin's mum had called Mrs Young to see what had happened.

"I'm so sorry," Mrs Young said. "Some of his school friends came to fetch him. I thought they were all going round to your house to play with Robin. And today I don't know where he's gone! He will

be in a lot of trouble when he
gets home.

"I just don't know what's wrong with him recently. I think these new school friends are a bad influence on him. But you tell Robin to stay positive. I'm sure we'll sort it all out."

Robin couldn't help being upset; he'd been good friends with Angus for a long time,ever since nursery school. They lived on the same street and used to play together at weekends, and often helped each other with their homework. But since the start of term, Angus had been ignoring Robin.

Sometimes he was rude to the teachers and had started to fall behind in class. His school uniform always looked scruffy, as if he had been getting into fights. He'd fallen in with the wrong crowd and wanted to impress them.

His mum kept telling him that those kids were a bad influence and would only get him into trouble, but he wouldn't listen.

Robin was waiting for Grandad's phone call to tell him that the car boot sale was cancelled, but it didn't come. Then suddenly ... Beep, beep, beep, beep! It was Grandad's little red car.

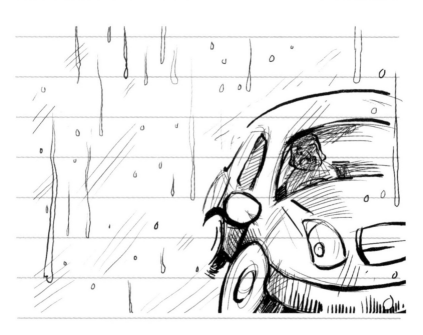

"Come on, Robin, it's Sunday morning. Time to go to the car boot sale."

"Grandad, it's so wet that I thought it would be cancelled today."

"Not exactly. It's been moved into the Church Hall."

So off they went.

"Here you are, Robin, here is your 50 pence to spend on a toy."

"Thank you, Grandad."

The hall was crowded with stalls and damp people; some of them had come to get out of the rain, because it was dry and warm inside.

"Okay, Robin, where shall we look first?"

"Oh, I'm not sure, Grandad. Let's wander around all the stalls and see what we can find."

So that's what they did.

"I know, Grandad, let's go and see Paul's stall. He usually has some interesting toys."

As the hall was so crowded, Paul didn't have his usual big stall.

"Today I have brought *Paul's Small Stall*," he joked, but it was still crammed with interesting things.

"I see," said Grandad. "So
we have *Paul's Small Stall in
the Tall Church Hall.*"

Grandad and Paul both chuckled.

Paul's stall was very popular. He was the local postman, so he knew everybody in town. And, because everybody knew that he had a stall at the car boot sale, he was always being given interesting things to sell.

Also, because *Paul's stall* rhymes, people liked to make up silly poems. Only the other day he had delivered a parcel to Nelly Knitwear, and when she had answered the door, she said,

"Hello, Paul, I hoped you
would call; I have something
here to sell on your stall.
It's an unwanted gift, a big
orange ball,
I have to admit, I don't like it
at all!
It's in the kitchen, if I recall,
I'll just go and get it, so wait in
the hall."

While Robin looked at the
toys, several people passed
by and made silly jokes about
Paul's orange ball. Robin looked
at lots of different toys, but

he was somehow attracted to a toy fish.

How unusual, he thought. I wonder what the world looks like to a fish. I bet that he has a good story to tell.

"What do you say, Grandad; do you think that the fish has a good story to tell us?"

"Hang on, Robin, let me have a quick word with him."

Grandad worked his magic.

"Well, Robin, I think he has lots to tell us. For instance, do you have any idea where fish go for a day out?"

Robin had to admit that he didn't.

"Today is the day you could find out."

"Alright, Mr Small Stall, how much is the fish?" Robin asked.

"Carlos the Cod is on special offer today, and as the weather is so bad you can have him for only 50 pence."

"Great! That's exactly what I have to spend."

"Shall I put Carlos in a bag?"

Grandad and Robin had a look around the rest of the car boot sale to see if they could find something for Grandma. When they couldn't find anything they liked, they ended up back at Paul's stall again.

"Back again?" asked Paul.

"Yes," said Grandad. "I've been looking for something for Mabel, but I just don't know what."

"Here," said Paul, "take her this."

Paul gave Grandad the orange ball.

"You can have it for free, I don't like it at all, I can't take one more joke about Paul's orange ball."

"Perfect," said Grandad. "She's been going on all week about buying an exercise ball for someone."

When they got back to Grandad's house and opened the door, the smell of baking wafted out.

"Hmmm! Coconut tarts!" said Robin.

"Yes, dear. I know they're your favourite!" Grandma said.

"Here you are, dear, I have a present for you," said Grandad, handing Grandma the bag.

"I don't believe it, Harry! You got this from the car boot sale? How much did it cost?"

"To be honest with you, dear, it was free."

"Well I never," said Grandma. "I have been looking for one of these to give to Nelly Knitwear for her birthday."

Then Grandma wandered off to find some wrapping paper for the orange ball.

Robin took Carlos the Cod out of the bag and put him on the kitchen table. Grandad cast his magic spell.

"Little toy, hear this rhyme,
Let it take you back in time,
Tales of sadness or of glory,
Little toy, reveal your story."

Carlos blinked one eye and then the other, wiggled his tail

and opened his big cod's mouth.

"Hello, who are you?"

"My name is Robin, and this is my grandad."

"Hello, Robin; hello, Grandad. My name is Carlos the Cod."

"Yes, Carlos, we already know. You are very brightly coloured. Are you a real cod?"

"Actually no, I am not a real cod. I am more of a mock cod, if you understand what I mean? But let's just say that I am a real cod, because it's easier to spell. C.O.D... Cod."

43

"I bet you have had an interesting life, Carlos. Why don't you tell us what it's like being a fish?"

"Alright, Robin. If you and Grandad are sitting comfortably, I shall tell you a bit about me and my fishy friends.

"Where I grew up, I had lots and lots of friends. We all used to get together to swim around. In case you didn't know, a group of fish is called a shoal.

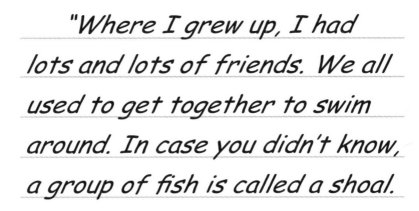

"I had known most of the fish in my shoal since I was born, and we all went to fish school together.

"Our mums never had to worry about us because we always did what we were told, and we looked after each other.

"One day, a new shoal of fish arrived in town. They were older than us, and I was really impressed by the way they would swim up to the surface while we were stuck at the bottom of the sea.

"One afternoon, a cod from the older shoal swam up to me

and introduced himself.

'What's your name, little codling?'

he asked.

" 'My name's Carlos,' I said.

'What's yours?'

" 'I'm Casper. Look, Carlos, don't you ever get bored of swimming around down here with the little fish?'

" 'Well yes, I do, Casper, but Mum and Dad won't allow me to go up to the surface. They say that it's dangerous.'

" 'We are going for a midnight swim,' he said. 'If you want to come with us, we will meet you at the sunken wreck at midnight.'

"I couldn't believe it.
Casper was a Cool Cod and he
had invited me on their swim!
I was going to be in with the
Cool Cod Crowd.

"I didn't say anything to Mum, but at dinner she said, 'I saw you talking to that naughty Casper Cod earlier. What did he want?'

" 'Oh nothing,' I answered. 'He was just telling me a joke about a jelly fish.'

" 'Carlos!' Mum said in her serious voice. 'I do not want you swimming around with that older shoal of fish. Do you understand me?'

" 'But, Mum...' I argued.

"But nothing! They're silly; they swim up to the surface and it's dangerous. You are not allowed to swim with them, do you understand me?'

"I went to my room in a mood. I wasn't going to let her ruin my chances of getting in with the in-shoal.

"I set my alarm for ten minutes to midnight, but as I was about to sneak out, Mum was waiting for me at the door.

"She made me go back to bed and I never got a chance to swim with the big fish.

"I hated her for ruining my life. The cool fish would never talk to me again and they'd think I was a baby.

"When I got up the next morning, Mum and Dad were getting ready for a day out.

"They'd packed some fish food and Dad was putting a film into the waterproof camera.

"I was confused; I thought I would at least be grounded.

" 'Where are we going?' I asked.

" 'We are taking you and some of your real friends to the Big Sea Aquarium, so that you can watch some strange creatures on the other side of the glass. They are called people

and we think that you may learn

something."

"Hmm, that's different,"
Robin said. "I had never
thought of fish watching people
before.
So what did you think of
them?"

"Well, Robin, if you listen to my story, you will find out.

"Mum and Dad had been before, but for me and my friends - Percy Plaice, Freddy Flounder, Henry Halibut and Peter Pollock - this was the first time.

"We were all getting very excited, and as soon as we arrived, we swam up to the glass to get a good look. What a curious and strange lot these people were.

"My friend Henry Halibut spotted a shoal of Punk Rockers.

" 'Hey, Carlos, look at that one,' he said. 'He's got a red and green fin on the top of his head. How strange is that?'

" 'I suppose it keeps his head straight when he's swimming.'

" 'If you think that's odd,' said Peter Pollock, 'just look at that poor person next to him. He can't be very well made; he's held together with chains and pins. What do you think is wrong with him?'

"I had to admit, I had no idea.

" 'Just imagine if we looked like that,' said Peter Pollock. 'They would call it cruelty to fish.'

" 'And look at that one,' said Percy Plaice. 'He's got a ring right through his nose. Do you think that's used to tie him down at night?'

"Again, I had to admit that I didn't know why he had a ring through his nose.

" 'What breed do you think they are, Carlos?' Percy Plaice asked.

" 'I don't know, but Dad thinks
they are a new and rare breed
called Punk Rockers.'

"Then I spotted something unusual: a group of children in school uniform. They were on a school trip and had managed to break away from the shoal leader. There were some bigger

kids all huddled around a much
smaller one, who had smoke
coming out of her mouth.

"I swam up to the glass
and shouted, 'Help her, help
her! She is on fire!' But they
couldn't hear me.

"My mum swam up behind me and said, 'She's not on fire, Carlos, she's smoking.'

" 'Smoking? Well, it looks really dangerous. Why is she doing it?'

"It is really dangerous, Carlos, and she probably knows that she shouldn't do it. But she's being naughty and doing it to impress the big kids.'

" 'Shall I try to get her to stop by tapping on the glass?' Henry Halibut asked.

" 'No, don't do that. The notice says: Do not tap on the glass; it may disturb the people.'

"So I swam away from the glass, knowing there was nothing I could do to help.

" 'Sorry, Mrs Cod,' said Freddy Flounder, 'I still don't understand why they do it.'

" 'No, me neither, Freddy.'

" 'Hey, gang,' Dad said. 'We are really lucky today; we are here for feeding time.'

" 'Do you think they would like some of our fish food?' asked Peter Pollock.

" 'No, don't be silly,' I said, pointing my fin at a big sign. 'That sign says: Do not feed the people.'

"We swam towards a family of people sitting together on a bench. On their laps they had packages wrapped in newspaper. Then they sprinkled salt and vinegar on the contents.

" 'What are they doing, Mum?' I asked.

" 'They're about to have their lunch,' she said. 'And do you want to know what they're having, Carlos? Well, I shall tell you anyway. They are having COD AND CHIPS!'

"I felt quite sick at the thought of it!

" 'And if you want to know how people catch fish, they wait until they swim up to the surface.'

"Now I understood that my mum had just been trying to protect me and stop me from doing something dangerous. I would never let older fish try to persuade me to do silly things ever again.

"It had been a fascinating day at the Big Sea Aquarium, but soon it was time to go home.

"Percy Plaice said, 'Okay, I have seen enough for one day, and people are staring at me. I don't like being looked at.

I came here to look at them, so I am going home.'

"Our fish gang hadn't realised that there were so many different types of people, with so many strange habits. We had all started the day not understanding anything at all about people. But by the end of the day we understood even less. It certainly was a different world on the other side of the glass.

"But we had all learned a very important lesson about listening to advice from our parents."

Carlos left a dramatic
pause.

Then he blinked that cod blink and waited for Robin's response to his story.

"Thank you so much, Carlos. It was very interesting to learn how you see people from your side of the glass.

"You know, only this morning I was looking out of the window at someone trying to light a cigarette in the rain, and I thought exactly the same thing as you. Why does she do it? I can't see any sense in it either."

"Yes," said Carlos. "Maybe she started when she was young, just like the girl in the aquarium, and now she can't stop. Thankfully for us, smoking has never caught on with fish."

All through Carlos's story, Robin couldn't stop thinking about how much this reminded him of what had happened to his friend Angus.

Robin decided that the best course of action would be to give Carlos to Angus as a present; maybe that way they could be friends again and Angus would learn a lesson before it was too late.

It was break-time at
school on Monday morning and
Robin had been looking
everywhere for Angus.

Eventually, he spotted
him behind the bike sheds,
huddled in the rain with a
group of older boys. As he got
closer, he could see cigarette
smoke and smell its horrid
smell.

"Angus!" he shouted.

Angus looked like he wanted to say hello, but a big boy shouted,

"Here comes the baby. Does he want to hang around with us big boys?"

Angus looked away.

Robin got closer and closer. The next thing he knew, he was flat on his face in the mud. One of them had pushed him in the back.

The big boys laughed ... all except Angus, who suddenly felt horribly guilty.

A teacher came to see what had happened and the older boys ran away.

Angus felt so guilty to have hurt a friend, especially one who was just being nice to him. He helped Robin to his feet and Robin gave him Carlos the Cod.

Carlos told Angus his story and Angus realised how horrible he had been to Robin, just so that he could fit in with the older boys. After class, they went back to Robin's house to do their homework together, just like they had always done.

It was a nice spring morning several days later when Postman Paul delivered some letters to Nelly Knitwear.

She opened the door and said, "Good morning, Paul Small Stall. Thank you for bringing my letters. This must be your lucky day. I have something special for your car boot stall."

Nelly handed Paul the big orange ball.

He smiled politely and said,
"Thank you, Nelly Knitwear, for
this big orange ball."

But deep down, he didn't
want it at all.